The NANNY GOAT'S KID

Jeanne Willis

Tony Ross

ANDERSEN PRESS

There was once a Nanny Goat, who wanted kids more than anything in the world.

But she couldn't have any of her own.

All the other goats had one.

Some even had two. It just wasn't fair.

"I'd be the best mum in the world," she sighed.

"Children are a pain," said her sisters. "They're noisy, naughty and they're always hungry."
"Mine wouldn't be like that," said the Nanny Goat.
"Don't kid yourself," said her sisters.

But the Nanny Goat still wanted a child.

And as she couldn't have any of her own . . .

. . . she adopted one.

"I don't care what it is as long as it's healthy," she smiled.

She didn't smile for long though. Nor did the Nanny Goat's Kid. He roared his head off from morning till night. He was noisier than any of her sisters' kids. Nobody got a wink of sleep.

"He's hungry," said her sisters. "Give him some grass. Kids love grass."

But the Nanny Goat's Kid wasn't like the others.

He spat the grass out.

He wouldn't eat hay. He wouldn't eat corn.
"She can't even feed him properly,"
whispered her sisters. "What
a bad mother she is!"

But the Nanny Goat never gave up. She tried
everything until she found something he liked.
"She spoils that kid," whispered her sisters.

The Nanny Goat's Kid grew big and strong.
A bit too big and a bit too strong.
The other kids were scared of him.
"He's only playing," said the Nanny Goat.

But her sisters didn't seem to think so.
"She lets him get away with murder," they bleated.

One by one, their kids went missing. The Nanny Goat's sisters blamed the Nanny Goat's Kid. "Was it you?" asked his mother.

The Nanny Goat believed him, but her sisters did not. They kicked him out of the herd. "You're not one of us. We don't trust you," they said.

"If he goes, I go!" said his mother. "He might not be my flesh and blood, but he's my son. I'll stand by him until the day I die."

"Don't stand too close!" said her sisters. "He'll be the death of you, you silly goat."

Off went the Nanny Goat and her kid into the wilderness.

But on the way, they met a huge tiger.

He crept out of his cave, grabbed the Nanny Goat and growled,
"I've got goat for my breakfast, goat for my lunch and now I've got
goat for my dinner!"

"That's not your dinner, that's my mother!" said the Nanny Goat's Kid. "And those are my cousins! They might not be my flesh and blood, but I'll stand by them until the day I die!"

With that, he smashed the cooking pot.

The tiger was so angry, he pounced on the Nanny Goat's Kid, but when he turned his back, the cousins put their heads together, butted the tiger and ...

. . . tossed him right over the moon.

When the Nanny Goat's sisters heard how the Nanny Goat's
Kid had saved the other kids, they welcomed him home.
"You've got a great kid there," they said.
"He's one of the family."

"That's my boy!" smiled the Nanny Goat.